Twinkle, Twinkle, Little Star

Illustrated by Dubravka Kolanovic

Published by Sequoia Children's Publishing,
an imprint of Phoenix International Publications, Inc.

8501 West Higgins Road, Suite 790
Chicago, Illinois 60631

59 Gloucester Place
London W1U 8JJ

www.sequoiakidsbooks.com

10 9 8 7 6 5 4 3 2 1

ISBN 978-1-64269-038-5

Twinkle was a little star. His mother was a Get Well star. His father was a Safe Journey star. Twinkle hoped he would grow up and have an important star job.

Mama Star said, "You will be a big star soon enough, Twinkle."

Papa Star said, "One day you will find the perfect job."

Twinkle hoped they were right. With a spin, he waved good-bye and went out exploring.

Twinkle wondered if he could be
a First Day of School star.

"I would help children be brave
and make friends. I would even
help them with their ABCs and
123s!" said Twinkle.

Twinkle wished he could be a Tie Your Shoes star.

"I would help children learn their left from their right, and teach them to make extra-tight knots and bows. I would help children keep from skinning their knees!" said Twinkle.

Twinkle thought that he could go
far as a Ride a Bike star.
"I would help children steer straight
and avoid busy streets. I could also
remind them to always wear a helmet,"
he said.

One night as Twinkle
sparkled in the sky, a little boy
said, "Look, Mama! I think that
star is twinkling just for me! I
will make a wish on that star."
He closed his eyes and said,

"Star light, star bright,
    First star I see tonight,
I wish I may, I wish I might,
    Have the wish I wish tonight."

"Mama! Papa!" cried Twinkle.
"I heard a wish! I heard a little boy
wish for a friend!"

Mama and Papa smiled. "It looks like
you are a Wishing star, Twinkle."

Twinkle was very happy. "What do I
do now?" Twinkle asked. "How will I
make his wish come true?"

"You will know," replied Mama
and Papa.

Twinkle sparkled brightly over the little wishing boy.

"To make a friend, you must look for someone who needs a friend, too. Just smile and say hello. Share a cookie. Be nice. But most of all, be yourself."

Twinkle grew up to be the very best
Wishing star. He even had a song!

Twinkle, twinkle, little star,
   How I wonder what you are.
Up above the world so high,
   Like a diamond in the sky.
Twinkle, twinkle, little star,
   How I wonder what you are!